Who's There, Spot?

Eric Hill

PUFFIN

Someone is at

the door, Spot.

Knock, knock!
Who can it be?

Tweet, tweet! Who is in the tree?

Ding, ding! Who is ringing the bell?

Giggle, giggle! Spot knows who's inside the playhouse.

Croak, croak! Who is in the pond?

Meow, meow!
Who is in
the basket?

Squeak, squeak! Who is in the cupboard?

Squawk, squawk! Who is in the

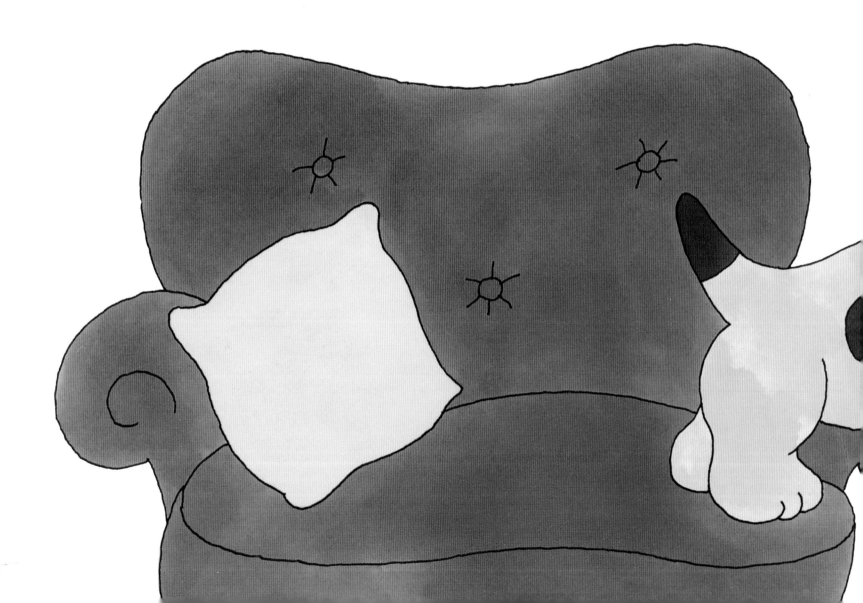

cage?

Splash, splash! Who is in the bath?

Did you enjoy

your day,
Spot?

Woof, woof!
It was fun.

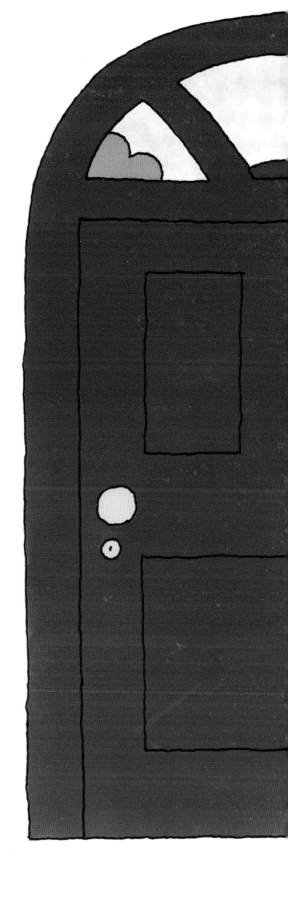

PUFFIN BOOKS

Published by the Penguin Group: London, New York,
Australia, Canada, India, Ireland, New Zealand and South Africa
Penguin Books Ltd, Registered Offices:
80 Strand, London WC2R 0RL, England

puffinbooks.com

First published by Frederick Warne and Co. 2005
Published in Puffin Books 2007
This edition published 2013

003

Copyright © Eric Hill, 2005
All rights reserved

The moral right of the author/illustrator has been asserted

Printed and bound in China

ISBN: 978–0–141–34375–4